This book belongs to

_____

_____

_____

Dedication

This book is dedicated to my mother Coral, my father Noel, my son Adam and my sister Tracey, whom I thank for their undivided support and encouragement and to all of my family and friends for patiently cheering me on.

A very special thanks to Kevin Watson of Blackstone Inks, (www.blackstone.ink) for kindly donating the beautiful range of Inks that I have used in the illustrations for this book.

And special thanks and acknowledgment to Dr. Kyle Jenkins, Dr. Beata Batorowicz (Creative Arts), David Martinelli (photography), Tony McLachlan (Graphics and Design), Catherine Wattiaux (Copyright), Shayla Olson and Mechelle Walker (Editing), who have so generously given their advice, time and professional experience whilst assisting me in the realisation of this Book.

Roz

Winter to Spring
in the Australian Bush

Written and Illustrated by

Roz Berg

Autumn's golden leaves are falling

The dams will soon turn brown

Platypus, Frilly and Kookaburra try to count

How many leaves have fallen to the ground

A breeze sweeps in and picks them up

Tumbling them through the air

They float along past Crowy Crow

While he is sitting there

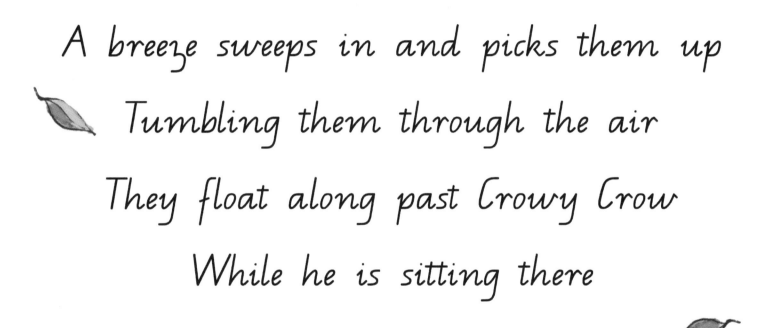

Everything is changing

If you look closely you will see

That even the pretty flowers

Are hiding from the Honey Bees

Winter's weather has now arrived

And everything feels so very cool

Goanna, Bluey, Maggie and Hare

Sit in the sun by the green rock pool

The grass that once was green is brown

Maggie sits quietly in the tree

Kangaroo and Emu look around

To find food and water for their families

Spiders and snakes find nice warm caves

Wombats burrow underground to sleep

Bats like to hang out upside down

Holding on with their little feet

Baby Emus sleep inside their eggs

Waiting to be born

It's usually in the Springtime

Sometimes in the early morn

Birds and Eagles fly up high

To catch the morning sun

Kangaroos jump and grasshoppers leap

To keep warm and have some fun

Possy Possum looks for food

But there's hardly any to be found

Sometimes he feels so hungry

His tummy grumbles really loud

Everyone is staying safe and warm

As the wind blows through the trees

In some places its so very cold

That it snows and you could freeze

But Springtime is what happens next

And the sun shines all gold and bright

Baby Roo peeks out from mummy's pouch

And Koala joeys hug each other tight

The rain will make the dams fill up

Flowers bloom and open their eyes

Ducks will swim and frogs will croak

And pretty colours will fill the skies

The leaves and branches all grow back

Dragonflies are flitting everywhere

Lorikeets and Fairy Wrens

Catch bugs right from the air

The birds are happy once again

They chirp and dance and sing

Kookaburras, Galahs and Cockatoos

Sit on the fence and flap their wings

Purple berries fill Lilly Pilly trees

You can see them hanging down

Honeyeaters eat the juiciest ones

Before they fall to the ground

Possy Possum finds an apple

He munches it to the core

When he's finished eating

He isn't hungry any more

Koaly Koala climbs up high

Into the blue gum trees

He sits on nice strong branches to

Eat the juicy eucalyptus leaves

Flowers bloom and grow and

Sway in the Springtime breeze

They smell so nice and pretty

And make pollen for the Honey Bees

The long awaited Springtime

Finally it's here

If you listen very closely

YOU can hear everybody CHEER!

Fun facts on the seasons and animals in this story.

Australia has 4 seasons
Summer: December to February.   **Winter:** June to August.
Autumn: March to May.   **Spring:** September to November.

Bats - The grey-headed flying fox is native to Australia and is known as a mega-bat. They are nocturnal (which means they sleep during the day) and search for food at night, eating pollen, nectar and fruit. They use their eyes and ears like we do and have the same night vision abilities as Cats.

Bilbies have big ears like rabbits and long pointy noses like bandicoots and are a marsupial. They have soft grey and white fur and white tipped black tails. They are nocturnal, don't need to drink water and eat spiders, termites, plant bulbs and grass seeds. They like hot, dry locations, dig and hide in deep spiral burrows through the day.

Echidnas or spiny anteaters are mammals who lay eggs. They can have long or short noses and are covered with hollow quills. They are only found in Australia and New Guinea and can live up to 50 years. They hibernate in winter in burrows. Their tongues can be 18cm long and they eat termites, ants and other soil invertebrates.

Frogs - The green tree frog can be found in eastern and northern parts of Australia. They like to hide in cool damp places, sometimes around your home. They eat insects, spiders, lizards, cockroaches and crickets.

Hares - Brown Hares originally come from Europe and Asia, they look like Rabbits but are bigger with black tips on their ears.

Kangaroos - There are millions of Kangaroos in Australia, some are known as the Eastern Grey and can be found in both southern and eastern parts of Australia.

Koalas live in one place in the world, Australia, and like Kangaroos their babies are also called Joeys. They climb trees and can eat 200 to 500 grams of Eucalyptus leaves each day.

Blue Tongue lizards live across most of Australia. They like open country with lots of cover like grass, rocks, logs and burrows.

Frilled neck Lizards are often called frilled dragons or frilled lizards and are commonly found in both Australia and New Guinea. Bearded dragons are a desert cousin of theirs.

Goannas - We have 25 different types of Goannas in Australia, most of them are carnivorous with sharp teeth and claws for hunting and eating. The largest one is the Perentie which can reach lengths of over 2.5m (8.2 ft).

Mouse - The long tailed field mouse eats plants, seeds, berries, fruits, insects and invertebrates such as snails, millipedes and grasshoppers and may even eat the flesh of other decaying animals.

Platypus is a semi-aquatic mammal that has a duck bill and a beaver like tail, webbed feet, fur like an Otter and lays eggs. It is only found in Australia in Queensland, New South Wales, Victoria and Tasmania and lives in Billabongs, small rivers and streams.

Possum - The common brush tail possum is nocturnal, has a thick bushy tail and lives all across Australia. They eat eucalyptus leaves, other leaves, berries and fruit and prefer to live in dense bush or tree hollows, they usually come out at night to eat.

Green Tree snakes are most commonly seen in backyards, parks and gardens during the day and live in Northern and Eastern Australia. They don't have fangs or venom and are more likely to slither away than bite you. They eat frogs, lizards, reptile eggs and geckos.

Carpet pythons are usually nocturnal and live in most parts of Australia excluding Tasmania. They live in the undergrowth or in tree branches and are often found in the roofs of buildings. They eat mostly after dark on smaller animals and can lay up to 20 eggs at a time.

Wombats – The hairy-nosed Wombat is the largest of the three Wombat species. They can weigh up to 32kg and be more than one metre long. They have softer fur, longer, pointier ears, a broad muzzle (nose), fine whiskers and eat native grasses.

Cockatoos – Sulphur-crested Cockatoos can live to be over 80 years old. They are highly intelligent and can be taught how to talk, dance and play games and can be very loud and mischievous. They like to live in trees in forests and bushland and eat seeds, grains, nuts, leaf buds, berries, fruit and vegetables.

Corellas belong to the Cockatoo family, they are smaller with white feathers on the top and yellow under their wings and tails. They have a blue ring around their eyes and pale pink between their eyes and beak. They live in hollow logs in large old gum trees and eat mostly grains and grass seeds.

Crows – The Torresian crow is glossy black and the one most often seen around homes in Queensland. Their eyes are white with a thin blue ring. They build round nests made of sticks and lined with grass high up in trees.

Ducks – The Australian Wood Duck is a dabbling duck found in most parts of Australia, commonly around dams and wetlands, eating grasses, herbs, clover and insects.

Eagles – Wedge-tails eagles are found throughout Australia, Tasmania and southern New Guinea. The largest wingspan ever verified for any eagle was for this species. A female eagle found in Tasmania in 1931 had a wingspan of 2.84m (9 ft 4 in) and was 1.06m (3ft 6in) long.

Emus live only in Australia and are the second largest bird in the world. Emus can sprint up to 48 km/h (31 mph) and eat fruit, seeds, plant shoots and insects and drink 9-18 litres of water per day.

Fairy-Wrens are the most extensive species in Australia. They prefer thicker forests or dense undergrowth and low shrubs. Every year the male superb fairy-wrens change colour from brown to blue. They eat insects and berries.

Galahs are also called rose breasted Cockatoos and are found in all Australian states. Sometimes they can be seen in large flocks of 500 or more.

Honey Eaters have a distinctive `brush-tipped` tongue which allows them to collect nectar and pollen from native flowers, they also eat a variety of insects and live in eucalypt forests and woodlands with blossoming trees.

Kingfishers are related to Kookaburras, they are beautiful, brightly coloured, shy birds that live near rivers, coasts and forests all over Australia. They eat fish, frogs, snakes, small animals, yabbies and insects. They can hover when fishing.

Kookaburras – In Australia we have the Laughing Kookaburra and the Blue-winged Kookaburra, both are large kingfishers. Laughing Kookaburras eat mostly insects, worms and shellfish and live in most parts of Eastern Australia. They like Eucalyptus trees, woodlands and open forests and can live up to 15 years.

Lorikeets – Rainbow Lorikeets live in Australia, they are very colourful Parrots with orange beaks. They are territorial and live in rainforests, coastal bush and woodland areas. Sometimes hundreds of them gather in the trees at Sunset.

Magpies are found in most parts of Australia and often form tribes of five to ten birds or more. They are territorial and protective of their homes. They like nesting in tall trees and sing at dawn and dusk.

Parrots – There are 56 different types of Parrots in Australia. They are brightly coloured birds like Mountain Parrots, Lorikeets, Rosellas and Budgerigars. The one we call Greenie is really a scaly breasted Lorikeet.

Winter to Springtime in the Australian Bush
Written and Illustrated by Rosalyn Berg
Published in Australia by Rosalyn Berg, Queensland
galleryrozberg@gmail.com

Printed by Golden Wattle Books, Toowoomba Queensland 2020

A catalogue record for this
book is available from the
National Library of Australia

Author/Illustrator: Berg, Rosalyn
Title: Winter to Springtime in the Australian Bush / Roz Berg
ISBN: 978-0-6487130-1-2 eBook: 978-0-6487130-2-9
Target Audience: Prep to Primary School Age
Subjects: Australian Animals, Seasons - Fiction

Born in Brisbane, Australia,
Rosalyn has had a life-long love of writing,
reading and art. She is currently undertaking
a Bachelor of Creative Arts with a focus on
painting and illustrating.

Roz has written a wide variety of poetry and
song lyrics and has been published in four Poetry Anthologies in the
USA.

Growing up on a bush property on the outskirts of Ipswich has
been the inspiration for this book.

In the early years the property was covered with a variety of
Eucalyptus trees and native flora and fauna including koalas,
kangaroos, possums, sugar-gliders and echidnas. In a billabong by
the creek lived two platypus that were a little shy if anyone went in
for a swim.

There were also beautiful birds and butterflies flying around the
property. This has led to a life-long love of nature and native
animals and has been the major influence for this book which we
truly hope you and your children enjoy reading.

CPSIA information can be obtained at www.ICGtesting.com
Printed in the USA
BVIW122211081220
595240BV00002B/2